Our Fri
FARM ANIMALS

Written by Stephanie C. Oda
Illustrated by Mike Peterkin

GALLERY BOOKS
An Imprint of W. H. Smith Publishers Inc.
112 Madison Avenue
New York City 10016

I t is morning on the farm.
"Cock-a-doodle-doo!" crows the rooster.
 Farmer Dan and all the farm animals wake up.
Today will be another busy day for our friends,
the farm animals.

"Moo, moo," says the cow. "Today
I'll moo, and I'll chew, and I'll give
Farmer Dan my fresh, creamy milk."

"Meow, meow," says the cat. "Today I'll prowl, and I'll yowl, and I'll scare the mice away from the barn."

"Neigh, neigh," says the horse. "Today I'll clip, and I'll clop, and I'll pull the big wagon full of hay."

"Baa, baa," say the sheep. "Today
we'll graze, and we'll laze on the
sweet, green grass in Farmer Dan's meadow."

"Woof, woof," says the dog. "Today
I'll guard and work hard to help
Farmer Dan round up the sheep and
bring them back home."

"Oink, oink," say the pigs. "Today
we'll dine and feel fine when we play
in the cool, squishy mud."

"Gobble, gobble," says the turkey.
"Today I'll gobble, and I'll gabble, and I'll
show off my fancy, fanned tail."

"Quack, quack," say the ducks. "Today we'll splish, and we'll splash when we go for a nice, long swim in the pond."

"Cluck, cluck," say the chickens. "Today
we'll pick, and we'll peck, and we'll lay
fresh eggs for Farmer Dan's breakfast."

Now it is evening on the farm. All the animals have done their work today and are happily eating their supper.

The day is over. It is time for everyone on the farm to sleep because tomorrow is another busy day for our friends, the farm animals.